DIRTY AND DANGEROUS JOBS

Arctic Trucker

By Joseph Gustaitis

Reading Consultant: Susan Nations, M.Ed.,
Author/Literacy Coach/Consultant in Literacy Development

Marshall Cavendish
Benchmark
New York

Published by Marshall Cavendish Benchmark
An imprint of Marshall Cavendish Corporation

Other Marshall Cavendish Offices:
Marshall Cavendish International (Asia) Private Limited, 1 New Industrial Road, Singapore 536196 •
Marshall Cavendish International (Thailand) Co Ltd. 253 Asoke, 12th Flr, Sukhumvit 21 Road,
Klongtoey Nua, Wattana, Bangkok 10110, Thailand • Marshall Cavendish (Malaysia) Sdn Bhd,
Times Subang, Lot 46, Subang Hi-Tech Industrial Park, Batu Tiga, 40000 Shah Alam, Selangor
Darul Ehsan, Malaysia

Marshall Cavendish is a trademark of Times Publishing Limited

All websites were available and accurate when this book was sent to press.

Library of Congress Cataloging-in-Publication Data
        Gustaitis, Joseph Alan, 1944-
            Arctic trucker / by Joseph Gustaitis.
        p. cm. — (Dirty and dangerous jobs)
        Includes index.
        ISBN 978-1-60870-169-8
        1. Truck drivers—Arctic regions—Juvenile literature. 2.
        Trucking—Arctic regions—Juvenile literature. 3. Vocational
        guidance—Juvenile literature. I. Title.
    HD8039.M795G87 2011
    388.3'2409709113—dc22   2009048391

Developed for Marshall Cavendish Benchmark by RJF Publishing LLC (www.RJFpublishing.com)
Editor: Amanda Hudson
Design: Westgraphix LLC/Tammy West
Photo Research: Edward A. Thomas
Map Illustrator: Stefan Chabluk
Index: Nila Glikin

Cover: A trucker drives on a snowy Alaskan highway.

The photographs in this book are used by permission and through the courtesy of: Cover: © Marvin Dembinsky Photo Associates/Alamy; 4, 20: AP Images; 5: © Danita Delimont/Alamy; 6: Doug Allan/The Image Bank/Getty Images; 8, 28: Photo courtesy Diavik Diamond Mines Inc.; 11: Alaskastock/Photolibrary; 12: AFP/Getty Images; 14: iStockphoto; 15: © Chris Boswell/Alamy; 16: Richard During/Stone/Getty Images; 18: © Alaska Stock LLC/Alamy; 21: Shutterstock; 22: Library of Congress Rep. #LOC LC-USZ62-34904; 24: photo by Jiri Hermann courtesy Diavik Diamond Mines Inc.; 26: Courtesy of *Ice Road Truckers* and © 2009 A&E Television Networks.

Printed in Malaysia (T).
135642

Words defined in the glossary are in **bold** type
the first time they appear in the text.

Hauling Freight

A trucker drives a load through the snow in Alaska.

"There have been a lot of times I didn't think I was going to live." That's how an **Arctic** trucker named Bill Vaughan once described his job.

He knew what he was talking about. Hundreds of truck drivers have died on the dangerous roads of the Far North. The Arctic region of North America contains riches—oil, diamonds, gold, and iron ore. It takes lots of equipment to get the riches out, things like earth movers, drills, pumps, and other machines. The mines, towns, and oil rigs also need lots of supplies—food, gasoline, housing materials, and other items. Arctic truckers haul all of these items.

Arctic truckers drive in conditions most people cannot even imagine. In the Arctic the temperature can sink to

70 degrees below zero Fahrenheit (57 degrees below zero Celsius). Sometimes it snows so hard a driver can't see. The wind can blow 50 miles (80 kilometers) an hour or more. One trucker saw the wind blow a rock the size of a baseball uphill—that's a strong wind! The roads can be very slick. They have dangerous curves and steep hills. The chances of a truck flipping over are great. Arctic truckers sometimes drive across frozen lakes. It is rare, but some trucks have fallen through the ice.

Most Arctic truckers are well paid, even though they work in an area where it can be hard to find jobs. Many truckers also enjoy the challenge of doing a hard job well. Others love the beauty of the Far North. Some own their trucks and like being their own boss.

Ice Roads

Most Arctic truckers drive on ice roads. As the name says, these roads are paved with ice.

Arctic truckers must be prepared to handle many different challenges along their routes.

Cat Trains

In the 1930s and 1940s in the Arctic, some freight haulers used **"Cat trains"** to get across frozen lakes and through the woods. Cat trains were made up of earthmovers built by the Caterpillar company. These earthmovers had plows in front and treads like a tank, which made them good for driving in the snow. Several of them were linked together to pull freight. They worked fine, but there was one major problem. They went only 3–4 miles (5–6 kilometers) per hour. That was much too slow to deliver supplies. It was necessary to find a way to use trucks. Trucks could deliver in one day what took a Cat train a month.

Earthmovers are good for driving in the snow, but they move slowly.

Sometimes an ice road is gravel or dirt in the summer but covered with ice in the winter. It is almost impossible to plow snow off a gravel or dirt road. It's easier to pack the road with ice. The ice creates a smooth surface much like a paved road. A tanker truck puts water on the road surface. When the water freezes, a machine called a **grader** comes along and packs the ice. Another machine then scratches the ice to leave a rough surface. The rough surface makes it easier for the tires to grip the road.

Some ice roads run mostly across frozen lakes. In the Arctic, it's common to find a long series of lakes that almost look like a chain when you see them on a map. These lakes are only a few miles apart. The ice road runs across each lake. To get from one lake to the next, trucks drive over a specially built land road, called a **portage**.

It's scary driving over frozen lakes. The trucker can hear loud cracking sounds. An Arctic trucker named T. J. Wilcox once said, "You can see air bubbles popping in the ice from the weight of the truck . . . and you're just like . . . 'I gotta get outta here'." Another driver, Jack Jessee, put it this way: "You're goin' slower, your heart beats a little faster."

The Eldorado Mine

The first ice road in Canada was built to supply a special mine. The road went from Yellowknife, a town in Canada's Northwest Territories, to what was known as the Eldorado Mine. This mine contained something very valuable—**uranium**. Uranium is the element used in nuclear power plants to make electricity. It is also used in nuclear bombs. After the United States entered World War II, the country started buying uranium from Eldorado. Scientists used that uranium to build the first atomic bomb. The uranium in the mine eventually ran out, but a silver mine opened in the same region. The ice road was still needed and is still used today.

7

Today, departments of transportation oversee many of the ice roads. Other ice roads are kept up by private companies that have special ice road skills. For example, a privately owned business takes care of the winter ice road in Canada's Northwest Territories.

When warm weather comes, the ice roads melt. In some areas, when that happens, people have no other roads. When the ice melts, all that's left is water, swamp, and **permafrost**, or ground that never completely thaws. It's almost impossible to build a road over swamps and permafrost. For that reason, driving a truck in the Arctic is mostly a winter job.

The Dalton Highway

One of the most famous ice roads is the James B. Dalton Highway in Alaska. It is also known as the "Haul Road."

Most Arctic truck driving is done in the winter.

The Dalton is used mostly to service the oil rigs on Alaska's **North Slope**. It begins just north of the city of Fairbanks. It runs 414 miles (666 kilometers) to the little town of Deadhorse near the Arctic Ocean. Just north of Deadhorse are the Prudhoe Bay oil fields, the largest oil fields in North America. The Dalton is a dangerous, tough road to drive.

Canadian Ice Roads

Canada has ice roads in several provinces, but they are especially important in the Yukon, the Northwest Territories, and Nunavut. Towns and mines in these areas rely on Arctic truckers for supplies. The trucks haul the construction equipment, generators, building materials, fuel, and food that make it possible for people to live in the Far North and for mines to operate.

One of the most famous Canadian ice roads is the Tibbitt to Contwoyto Road. It is partly in the region of northern Canada called the Northwest Territories and partly

An Ice Road in Siberia

Ice roads are not found only in North America. They also exist in countries in northern Europe, including Finland, Norway, and Sweden. The rugged Russian region of Siberia has many. One Siberian ice road is on Lake Baikal, the deepest lake in the world. Lake Baikal has a large island called Olkhon Island, which has become popular with tourists. It is about 3 miles (5 kilometers) from the shore. In the summer, people get to Olkhon by ferry. In the winter an ice road is built. Heavy trucks and other vehicles use the ice road to get to the island. When spring comes, the ice starts to get thin. Big trucks can't cross the ice safely. However, some people still walk or ride motorcycles across the ice to the island. This is dangerous because travelers never know if the ice is going to be thick enough to hold them.

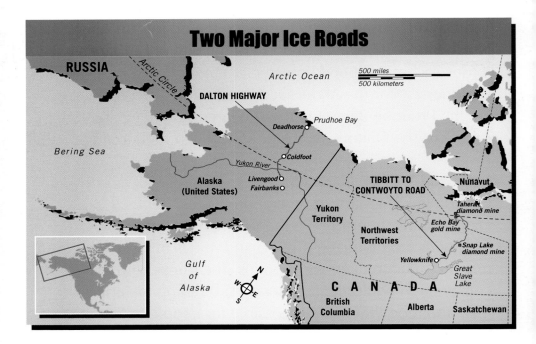

Two Major Ice Roads

in the territory in northern Canada called Nunavut. The road is 353 miles (588 kilometers) long, and most of those miles are on frozen lakes. Between lakes the truckers drive over 64 portages. The road supplies some rich diamond mines. Arctic truckers haul about 300,000 tons of equipment to the mines every year. When the spring thaw comes, there is no ice road. There is no road of any kind. It's important to haul as much freight in the winter as possible.

Which Is Worse?

It's hard to say which is more dangerous—driving on frozen water or driving on an ice road on land. On frozen water, an Arctic trucker has to worry about falling through the ice. But on land, the trucker has to worry about getting over high mountains or driving into a deep ditch at the edge of the road. Both options are pretty scary.

Staying Alive

It is easy for a truck to lose traction on a road with hills or sharp curves.

On the Dalton Highway, Arctic truckers say there are only two kinds of drivers: the ones who have gone into a ditch and the ones who are going to do it someday. Usually the road is safe, but when snow falls, it can become slick. The Dalton has a hill so steep it is known as the "Roller Coaster." The road also has many sharp twists and turns. Often a truck will lose traction on a curve or a hill. If a truck's tires start to spin out while the truck is going uphill, the truck will slide backward. There is a way to get out of this jam, but it takes skill. The trucker has to shift into the correct gear and work the brakes just right—not too hard,

Preventing Avalanches

The Dalton Highway has a section called "**Avalanche** Alley," where steep slopes line the side of the road. In an avalanche, a large amount of snow suddenly falls from the side of a steep mountain. The snow can bury a truck that happens to be on that part of the highway when the snow falls. So avalanche control experts in Alaska try to get snow off the slopes before an avalanche happens. After a heavy snowfall, they fire a big gun into the mountain. The shot makes the snow fall. Then plows push the snow away.

Avalanche control experts fire a gun into the mountains to make the snow fall.

not too light. When a truck's wheels spin, they polish the ice. This makes the ice even slicker and more dangerous for the next Arctic trucker.

The Tundra

Toward the north end of the Dalton, Arctic truckers reach the area known as the **tundra**. The Alaskan tundra is a vast plain where the **subsoil** is permanently frozen. Only mosses, short shrubs, and other low plants grow here. There are no tall trees to help slow down the wind. High winds can cause **white-outs**, which truckers call a "blow." Because truckers can't see, they might drive off the road and be buried in snow. There is also the risk of hitting an oncoming truck.

On both sides of the road are tall metal poles called "**snow poles**." They are often brightly colored to stand out against the snow. When heavy snow is falling, drivers look for these poles to make sure they are still on the road. Sometimes they can hardly see the poles. A driver named Kenny Jones once drove in a storm where, he said, "you could barely see the end of your hood." One driver drove off the road and crashed through the windshield. The glass ripped off his clothes. It was 40 degrees below zero Fahrenheit (70 degrees below zero Celsius) outside. He quickly froze to death.

At the north end of the Dalton, the trucker reaches Deadhorse. This community of fewer than 50 people is the closest town to the oil rigs at Prudhoe Bay. To get to the oil rigs farther north, an Arctic trucker actually drives on the sea ice. The driver can hear the ice cracking under the wheels of the truck.

Danger: Frozen Lakes

When Arctic truckers drive on frozen lakes, one of the worst things that can happen is to break through the ice. Often, the first truck just cracks the ice. The next truck is the one that falls through. Usually, drivers are able to jump out before they sink. Some truckers drive with their left hand on the door handle. This way the trucker can open the door fast if the truck starts to sink. The trucker can jump onto the ice before the truck goes down. The ice might not be able to hold up a heavy truck, but it can hold up the driver. It's said that a trucker who goes into the water will freeze to death in 45 seconds.

Using the Chains

On the Dalton, when the road gets slick, drivers have to put a heavy set of chains on the four front tires. Chains are especially useful on the steep slopes of mountains. There's an art to putting on chains. If they are too loose, the chain links can start to break. If they are too tight, they can damage the tires.

Heavy chains help tires grip the road in icy weather.

Only low plants can grow in the frozen ground of the Alaskan tundra.

But a truck that falls through the ice is not lost forever. It can later be towed out. A truck can stay in the cold water for months and still be able to be repaired. One builder of ice roads used to call the trucks that stay under water "cold storage."

Falling In

On one freezing day in the late 1960s, a truck driver named Al Frost was steering across the ice of Great Bear Lake in Canada. He was driving a vehicle called a Bombardier. All of a sudden he felt the rear end drop through the ice. He jumped out and landed where the ice was thick enough to hold him. The Bombardier sank about 15 feet (4.6 meters). Objects began to float up from the vehicle. Frost was able to get a case of pork chops, a teapot, and a blanket. In his pocket, he had two books of matches that he used to build a fire. He boiled the pork chops in the teapot. Frost survived for eight days before a plane spotted him and picked him up. He later said, "I had lost a few pounds but I did feel pretty healthy."

Challenging the Arctic

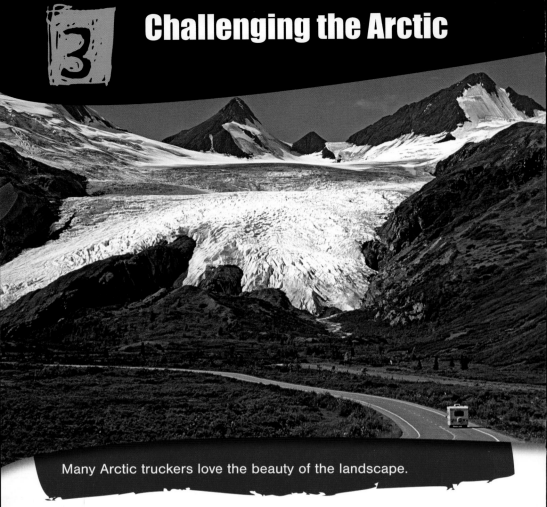

Many Arctic truckers love the beauty of the landscape.

An executive at an Alaskan trucking company once said that being an Arctic trucker is "the most difficult trucking job in America and perhaps the world. . . . Every trip," he said, "is an adventure and a challenge." Many Arctic truckers actually like the challenge of their job. They feel that a driver who can handle an ice road is in a special group of truckers. As one trucker from southern Canada put it, "Nobody back home has done anything like this." Arctic truckers are considered some of the best in the business. An Alaskan trucker, for example, can usually get a job easily in the lower 48 states.

The Beauty of the North

Some Arctic truckers love the beauty of the landscape. Even though the area is cold and dangerous, they wouldn't want to be anywhere else. A writer named Jim Christy, who spent a lot of time on Alaska's highways, feels very attached to the area. "There is no other place on earth like it," he says. "If you have spent considerable time here, as I have, it keeps tugging at you when you are gone. . . . [It] is heartbreakingly beautiful." One person from a company that helps drivers find jobs says that Arctic truckers "see things others wouldn't see in a normal job—bears, wildlife, amazing scenery."

Trucking Companies

Many Arctic truckers do not own their own trucks. Buying and operating a truck is expensive. Just filling up the fuel tank can cost more than a thousand dollars. Many drivers work for trucking companies that own the trucks.

The people who run trucking companies know that it takes a special person to be an Arctic trucker. Carlile Transportation Systems is one of the biggest trucking companies in Alaska. It operates about 200 trucks, many

Arctic Fever

The Arctic explorer Robert E. Peary once said he had "Arctic fever" in his veins and could never get rid of it. Peary explored the Arctic more than 100 years ago. Since then, people have been using the term "Arctic fever" to describe their love of the Far North. The fever still gets people today. Many people want to make adventurous trips to the Arctic—and they do!

It can cost more than a thousand dollars to fill the fuel tank of a large truck.

on the Dalton Highway. To get a job at Carlile, a trucker has to take a medical exam. The company then tests truckers on a simulator. The simulator is a full-size truck cab that gives the driver the same sensation as driving on an actual road. The drivers who pass the simulator test are then given a week of "basic training."

Preparing the Truck

Part of the job of an Arctic trucker is getting the truck ready. The trucks they drive are a lot like the trucks people would see anywhere else. But most trucks come from the factory with an "Arctic package," which means they have thicker **insulation** and windows with double panes of glass. Then, the drivers do other things to the trucks. They usually add a "**winter front**." This is a quilted shield that goes over the front grille. It keeps the engine warm and protects against flying rocks. Next, the trucker wraps the truck's lines and pipes with special insulation to protect against freezing.

Once a trip is started, the trucker tries never to turn off the engine. The bitter cold might make it impossible to

Ice Road Truckers

One of the most surprising recent hits on television was a show called *Ice Road Truckers*. When the History Channel first put it on the air in 2007, more than 3 million people watched. *Ice Road Truckers* is a reality TV show that follows real truckers as they drive through the Arctic. In the first two seasons, the truckers drove on Canada's frozen lakes. In the 2009 season, they tackled Alaska's Dalton Highway. They drove through storms, over high mountains, and around dangerous curves. Some real truckers thought the show made Arctic trucking look more dangerous than it really is, but TV viewers loved it.

start the engine again. It takes at least 13 hours to drive the Dalton Highway. It can take much longer if the weather is bad or if the truck has mechanical problems.

A "winter front" is a quilted shield that protects the truck's front grille and keeps it warm.

Truckers must make sure that their loads are balanced and tied down well.

A trucker also must take good care of the truck's **cargo**. The weight of whatever the truck is carrying has to be balanced just right. An uneven load—too much weight on one side of the truck—can cause the truck to tip over on a curve. If a truck is carrying a load of pipes and the pipes are not tied down well, a pipe might come loose. That pipe might crash into the cab of the truck and badly hurt or even kill the driver.

21

On the Job

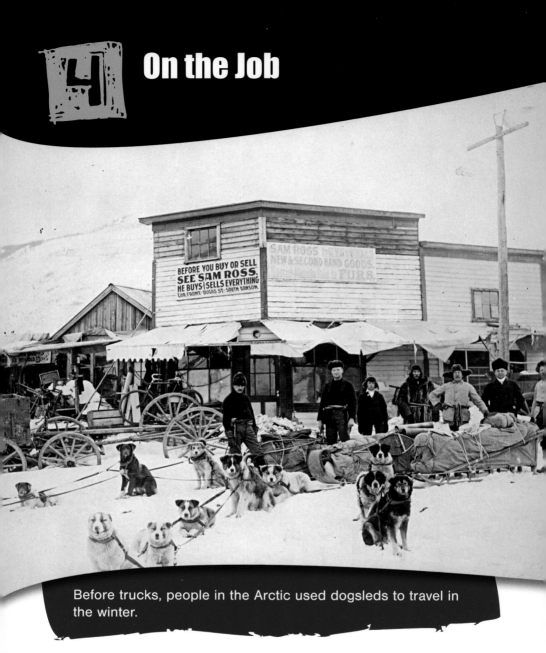

Before trucks, people in the Arctic used dogsleds to travel in the winter.

In the early 1900s, people in the Arctic traveled in the winter mostly by dogsled. In the summer, they used wagons pulled by horses. By the 1930s many products were being brought out of the Far North—furs, lumber, and ore from mines, for example. Alaska was found to have large amounts of coal, sand, and gravel, which are all heavy and bulky. As early as the 1930s, Alaska was producing some oil. After World War II (1939–1945), a lot of oil and natural gas was found. It takes a lot of equipment to operate oil and natural gas fields. It became necessary to find a better way to haul materials in and out. Using airplanes was too expensive. Eventually, people began to build ice roads. The era of the Arctic trucker was born.

Hard Work, Good Pay

Some Arctic truckers are paid very well. In 2009, drivers on the Tibbitt to Contwoyto Road in Canada were earning hundreds of dollars a day. The drivers are given extra money for food and expenses. Many drivers on the Dalton Highway are paid by the load, so the more they drive, the more money they make. They can make a lot. Experienced drivers earn more than beginners. Drivers who haul extra-wide loads earn even more.

Companies that hire Arctic truckers warn drivers who want to take the job only because the money is good. To earn that money, the companies say, drivers have to be able

Ice Road Pioneer

One of the first builders of ice roads in Canada was John Denison, a former member of the Royal Canadian Mounted Police. In 1947, a company named Byers Transport hired him to build an ice road from Edmonton, Alberta, to its mines near Yellowknife in the Northwest Territories. Denison became famous for proving that ice roads could be built in very rugged places. These were places where others thought it was impossible to build an ice road. A book about his adventures, *Denison's Ice Road*, was published in 1975.

Hauling a Wide Load

Driving an extra-wide load is a special skill. A "pilot car" drives ahead of the truck to warn oncoming traffic that an extra-wide load is coming. Sometimes the pilot car breaks down and the trucker has to drive alone. A trucker always drives very slowly when carrying an extra-wide load. It can take four or five days to haul an extra-wide load the length of the Dalton. A regular truck can make the trip in about 13 hours. An extra-wide truck will try to move over when a truck is coming the other way. But that can put the driver at risk of going off the road.

A trucker must drive very slowly when carrying an extra-wide load.

to do a really tough job. All trucking jobs have challenges. Most truckers are away from their families for long periods of time. They can risk their health by getting little exercise and eating unhealthy food on the road. They have to be able to stay awake for many hours, often driving through the night.

Arctic truckers face those challenges and more. They must be able to steer a truck with a really heavy load over slick ice. They have to be able to stop a large truck if it starts to slide on an icy hill. An Arctic trucker also has to know how to take care of the truck and to get out and repair it in a snowstorm. It's not an easy way to make money.

Off Season

When the season is over, the ice truckers return home. Some take trucking jobs where they live. Some take jobs that don't involve trucks. Most Arctic truckers live in either Canada or Alaska, however. Living there helps them get used to the weather and to driving in wintry conditions.

Although few truckers on the Dalton own their own trucks, elsewhere in Alaska and Canada many drivers do own their own trucks. Often, these drivers are people who just like trucks and like being on the road. One of them said, "I've done everything else there is to do, and there's nothing I've ever loved more than truck driving." As with truck drivers elsewhere, they like feeling independent. They don't have anyone telling them what to do.

Not Just for Men

Some people might think that Arctic trucking is a job just for men, but some Arctic truckers are women. One of them, Lisa Kelly, has appeared on the TV series *Ice Road*

The number of female truckers is growing. Lisa Kelly has appeared on the TV show *Ice Road Truckers*.

Truckers. She lives in Wasilla, Alaska, and drives on the Dalton. "I really enjoy it," she says. "I like the freedom of getting out and not having a boss directly there." A truck driving school in Anchorage, Alaska, recently started its first all-women class.

In general, the number of female truckers is growing. According to the American Trucking Association, in 1995 there were 130,000 female truck drivers in the United States. In 2005, there were 155,000.

The Future of Ice Roads

Some people are worried about future of the ice roads. Global warming, or the slow increase in worldwide temperatures, is causing Arctic winters to get shorter. Before 1991 the ice roads in the Alaskan tundra opened in early November. Now they open in January. In the past, ice roads in the Canadian province of Manitoba were usable about 60 days a year. In some recent years, they were usable for only 20 days or so. In 2006 the ice road season ended early in Canada's Northwest Territories because the weather turned warm. Mining companies had to spend $100 million shipping cargo on planes.

In the future, if the season is too short, many ice roads might not be worth building. How will people and

Drive the Dalton Yourself

You don't have to be a trucker to drive the Dalton Highway. There aren't many places to stop, but a driver in a passenger car can get from Fairbanks to Prudhoe Bay in about two days. Almost everyone who makes this trip does it in spring or summer. In the winter, 90 percent of the traffic is truck traffic.

Global warming is causing Arctic winters to get shorter. This
has created problems for ice roads.

companies in the Arctic get their supplies? Replacing ice roads with other kinds of roads that can be driven year-round would cost billions of dollars. Shipping goods by airplane costs six to eight times as much as shipping by trucks. Some people think that suppliers will be able to use **hovercrafts** in the future. A hovercraft is a vehicle that moves over water or land on a cushion of air created by fans. Another possible solution would be using airships, or **blimps**. A blimp is an aircraft that is lighter than air. Its large balloon is usually filled with helium.

Trucking will not disappear from the Arctic. There will still be gravel and paved roads in the Far North. But many people will be disappointed if the ice roads start to disappear and if the great days of Arctic trucking slip into the past.

So You Want to Be an Arctic Trucker

Trucking companies prefer to hire drivers who are high school graduates and have clean driving records. This means that a driver has not gotten many tickets and has no history of drinking and driving.

In the United States, drivers need a Commercial Driver's License (CDL). To get one of these licenses, a person needs to pass a written test and a driving test. A truck driving school can help a driver prepare for the tests. A driver also has to pass an exam given by the U.S. Department of Transportation. Canada has similar requirements.

Drivers looking for work often search online for companies that are hiring Arctic truckers. The website "Canadian Truckers" has names of Canadian companies that hire truck drivers. The Canadian immigration office accepts requests from non-Canadians who are looking for truck driving jobs in Canada.

GLOSSARY

Arctic: The area of the Earth at or around the North Pole.

avalanche: A sliding of a large amount of snow down the side of a mountain.

blimp: An aircraft that is lighter than air and propels itself.

cargo: Goods carried by a large vehicle.

Cat train: A system of freight hauling that uses earthmovers built by the Caterpillar company.

grader: A machine used to surface and repair roads.

hovercraft: A vehicle that rides over land or water on a cushion of air.

insulation: A material that is used to protect against heat or cold or to deaden sound.

North Slope: The region of Alaska that borders the Arctic Ocean. The North Slope contains the valuable Prudhoe Bay oil field.

permafrost: Ground that is permanently frozen.

portage: A road or path between two bodies of water.

snow pole: A marker placed at the side of an Arctic highway to help the driver locate the edge of the road when the ground is covered with snow.

subsoil: The layer of soil that is just below the surface.

tundra: A treeless area in the Arctic where the soil is often frozen. The tundra supports low-growing plants like moss and small shrubs.

uranium: A metal that is used for nuclear fuel in power plants that make electricity and is used in nuclear weapons, such as atomic bombs.

white-out: A weather condition in which the wind blows snow through the air, making it difficult to see.

winter front: A quilted shield that goes over the front grille of a truck to keep the engine warm and protect against flying rocks.

TO FIND OUT MORE

BOOKS

Guigon, Catherine. *The Arctic*. New York: Abrams Books for Young Readers, 2007.

Kupperberg, Paul. *The Alaska Highway*. New York: Chelsea House, 2009.

Somervill, Barbara A. *Alaska*. New York: Children's Press, 2008.

Turnbull, Andy. *By Truck to the North*. Toronto: Annick Press, 1998.

WEBSITES

http://www.blm.gov/ak/st/en/prog/recreation/dalton_hwy.html
On this site from the U.S. Bureau of Land Management, you can download a visitor's guide to the Dalton Highway.

http://www.dot.gov.nt.ca/_live/pages/wpPages/Winter_and_ice_roads.aspx
This website explains all about ice roads. You can even view a brochure on how to build an ice road.

http://www.thedieselgypsy.com/Ice%20Roads-3B-Denison.htm
This site, called "Ice Roads of Canada," has lots of good pictures of John Denison building one of the early ice roads.

About the Author Joseph Gustaitis is a freelance writer and editor living in Chicago. He is the author of many articles in the popular history field. After working as an editor at *Collier's Year Book*, he became the humanities editor for *Collier's Encyclopedia*. He has also worked in television and won an Emmy Award for writing for ABC-TV's *FYI* program. He is the author of *Chinese Americans* in Marshall Cavendish Benchmark's *New Americans* series and of the book *Storm Chaser* in the *Dirty and Dangerous Jobs* series.